Night Visitors

Claire Daniel
Illustrated by Ellen Beier

Rigby

Contents

1

A Family Secret

Long past my bedtime, a knock at the front door woke me. I heard my father's booming voice yell out, "Who's there?"

"Friends," a stranger's voice answered. My father opened the door and went outside, and the front door closed quietly behind him.

I slipped from my bed to the window and strained to see what was happening outside. The moon was only a tiny sliver, so I peered out the front window into the darkness. I looked toward the road through the oak trees that spotted our grassy lawn, but there was no movement there. Then I looked out the window on the left side of the house. I saw my father and another man walking quickly toward the old well.

To my surprise, my dog Gus ran to the stranger and wagged his tail. The man took a moment to pet him, then he motioned toward the forest. Three other people emerged from the forest. One of them appeared to be a small child. The three people climbed into the well and disappeared. The man who had motioned to them shrank back into the forest, the darkness swallowing him. My father walked back into the house with our dog in tow, shutting the door behind him. Then all was quiet, as if nothing had happened.

The next morning, my mother prepared a larger than usual breakfast. She baked dozens of biscuits and stacked fried eggs on large platters. My little brother Samuel was only seven and didn't notice anything unusual. I ate quietly and wondered how to ask my question. Then I said, "Mother, who were those people I saw last night?"

She tossed me a startled look, then said, "Later, Amelia." She looked over at my father and he nodded. "When Samuel and I go to the store this morning, your father will speak to you."

"But . . ." I protested.

"Later," my father said sternly. I looked at him, his kind face firmly set.

"Yes, Papa."

An hour later, my father spoke to me quietly and simply. I remember feeling so proud that he felt I was old enough to understand and to be trusted with our dangerous family secret.

2

The Underground Railroad

My father and mother owned a store in Kennett Square, about two miles from our house. It was called a general store because customers could get almost anything there. We sold lace, bolts of cotton and wool, and some ready-made clothes, too. Most of the time, we had a good supply of staples like sugar and coffee. In short, we stocked everything from turpentine to flour. In the warm months, the store was full of fresh produce like carrots, potatoes, and green beans. And, of course, we always had candy for the children.

On that particular fall morning of 1852, my mother opened the store. After I washed up the breakfast dishes, my father led me to the parlor for our talk. I listened very carefully, and felt quite grown-up to be trusted with everything he told me.

"You know your mother and I feel that slavery is wrong," he began.

"Yes," I said. I knew that southern states had

slaves, and that our state of Pennsylvania did not.

"Slave owners can treat slaves any way they wish because they are regarded as property. We feel that slavery is cruel and immoral," Papa said. I nodded. I had heard my parents speak of this many times.

Then he went on to explain that some slaves were treated well and had plenty to eat and enough clothing to protect them from the cold. But he also said many slave owners fed and clothed their slaves poorly and often beat them to keep them from causing trouble. He explained that in the early days of slavery, some of the more courageous slaves attempted to escape from their owners, but most were caught, then returned and punished severely. The lucky ones got away. I knew some of what Papa was telling me, because I had listened to him talk to my mother about it many times. Still, I listened closely and looked him straight in the eyes.

Then he said simply, "We are part of the Underground Railroad."

"What is an underground railroad?" I asked.

"The Underground Railroad is a way that slaves can escape to the northern states and into Canada, where there is no slavery. The Underground Railroad is a railroad without engines, railroad cars, smoke, or metal. It's made up of people, routes that crisscross, and secret hiding places," Papa explained.

"Our house is what's called a 'safe house.' A safe house is a hiding place for escaped slaves. It's also called a 'station.' Other hiding places might be a barn or a church. The slaves are given food and clothing at a station. People who shelter, feed, and clothe the escaping slaves are called 'stationmasters.'"

"So we are stationmasters?" I asked.

"Yes, Amelia, we are," he said, "but we are only a small part of the Railroad."

He paused and then went on. "Your mother and I are workers on the Railroad. We use the cover of darkness and secret signals as tools to do our work. Do you understand?"

"Yes, Papa, I think so."

"We must keep the Underground Railroad a secret or we could endanger those who try to escape. We can't help the slaves if we are found out."

"But we live in Pennsylvania," I protested. "Isn't this a free state?"

"It is," he agreed. "But even though slavery is against the law here, it is still legal for slave owners in other states to come to Pennsylvania and capture runaway slaves and return them to another state."

"Does that mean it's against the law to help slaves

to freedom?" I asked. "Are we breaking the law when we help?"

My father nodded. "Yes, Amelia, we *are* breaking the law. But we believe slavery is wrong. Instead, we are following our belief that every human being deserves to be free." Then he asked quietly, "Are you afraid of breaking the law?"

I was worried that something would happen to my mother and father, but I knew that what he said was right. So I said, "No, Papa."

Then I quickly added, "Will you let me be a worker on the Railroad?"

He sighed and said, "Amelia, you already are. By keeping silent, you are helping. Perhaps you can help your mother a little more around the house."

"Yes, Papa!"

I was bursting with questions. "How did the Underground Railroad get its name?"

"No one really knows," my father said, "but they say there was once a slave named Tice Davids who was mistreated by his slave master and longed to be free. One day he finally managed to escape and travel for many, many miles. All the while, his slave master was right behind him.

"Alone, Tice ran through the woods, jumping over

bushes and weaving through the trees. He was running north, searching for the Ohio River, the only thing that separated him from freedom. Finally, he spotted the river. Without hesitation, he dove into it, and swam as fast as he could. His master followed close behind Tice in a rowboat. Tice finally reached the other side of the river and ran. His master took his eyes off Tice for only a moment as he landed the boat on the shore. When he looked up, Tice had disappeared. The slave owner searched and searched, but he couldn't find a trace of Tice. Finally the master decided his slave must have escaped on an underground road!"

"So how did 'railroad' become part of the name?" I asked.

"When the escape paths began to crisscross the country like train tracks, people called it the Underground Railroad," my father explained.

I stopped to think. My parents had fed and clothed people I did not know. Then I thought of the clothes that I had outgrown. They had mysteriously disappeared. Perhaps some young girl was walking to freedom in the very clothes I had worn! I grinned. "Is that where my old dresses and shoes have gone?"

"Yes—little girls are wearing clothes you've outgrown. And many times I've given away new clothes and supplies from the store," Papa replied. "Do you know what 'free-labor goods' means?"

I thought about these words, but I wasn't sure of their meaning, so I shook my head.

"'Free-labor goods' are products that are made by free men. These are the only products I will sell. I won't help the people who use slaves or companies that sell products that are made by slaves."

"Do the noises I hear in the cellar belong to slaves on their way to freedom?"

Papa nodded.

I asked, "Why do they climb in the old well? You've told Samuel and me to stay away from it."

"There's a tunnel that goes from the well to our cellar. That's how they get into the house," Papa replied.

Suddenly I understood. Behind our house was a heavily wooded area. The old well could be seen from my bedroom window. To the right of the old well was the new well, and behind that was the barn and more woods and forest. Now I understood how the people got into the cellar.

But there was still much I wanted to know. "How do the slaves know where to go?" I asked.

"People lead the escaping slaves from station to station. These people are called 'conductors,'"

Papa explained.

"Do the escaping slaves have a name, too?"

My father nodded. "They are called 'cargo.'"

I hesitated before I asked the next question. "Why do people have slaves in the first place?"

My father took a deep breath and sighed. Then he said, "Many people depend on slaves to help them make money. Farmers in the South need cheap labor to pick cotton, and the northern factories need the cotton to make cloth. Many people think they need the slaves to make a living."

"But what about the slaves? Do they get paid for the work they do?" I wondered.

"No. They get paid nothing for the work they do."

"But they do most of the hard work. Why can't people pay them?" I asked.

"Owners of large farms don't think they can make enough money if they pay people to help them raise and pick the crops."

"I don't think it's right for one person to own another," I said. "Couldn't we talk to people and change their minds?"

My father looked at me with concern. Then he said quietly and sternly, "No, Amelia. That is one thing you must not do. If we are to help the slaves who wish to be free, we must keep our opinions to ourselves. Then the people we help will be safer. And we will be free to save more people." He paused and added, "Do you understand?"

"No, sir," I said. "Why can't we get our friends to help, too? If we have more people to help the slaves escape, wouldn't it be better for everyone?"

"Not now," he replied. "Secrecy is the best tool we can use to help these people. If anyone knows what we're doing, then we'll be forced to stop. Besides that, we might be arrested. Do you understand?"

"Yes, Papa."

"Will you promise not to say a word to anyone? Even if you suspect they're working on the Underground Railroad as well?"

"There are other people we know who are working on the Railroad?"

My father didn't answer. Instead he insisted, "Do you promise?"

His stern look frightened me, so I decided not to question him anymore. I simply answered, "Yes, Papa."

Then he added, "Your brother is too young to keep a secret like this, so we won't tell him. He might let it slip out at school or while he's playing with his friends. Then we couldn't help anyone."

"What could happen if we got caught helping a slave escape?" I asked hesitantly.

My father got up from his chair and patted me on the arm. "You are not to worry about that, because it won't happen. As long as we're careful, everything will be fine."

And that was all my father would say about the matter. And so I began my work on the Underground Railroad, with my most important job as secret keeper.

3

Keeping a Secret

The next day I listened carefully and became aware of the slaves in the house. Just before dark, I heard their quiet movements and voices under the floorboards in the parlor. I asked my mother if I could talk with them or take them food, but she insisted that I could not. Before the evening meal was served, I noticed that she took a platter full of ham, biscuits, and butter beans to the parlor.

The following night I didn't hear the slaves leave. Before I went to bed, I peered out into the dark night. I looked at the stars shining brightly overhead and shuddered. It was cool that night. Soon I would be in my warm, cozy bed. Would the slaves be so comfortable? I hoped so, and I wished them well.

A month later, I had a big scare at school. I was eleven, and was in my fifth year, but we had students of all levels in the classroom. I was studying my spelling words as the younger children had their lessons.

The lecture began as usual. Mr. Simpson, our teacher, was telling the smaller children about the invention of the steam engine.

"This invention has changed the lives of everyone in this country," he said.

Mr. Simpson placed pictures of a steamboat and a train on the chalk rail. Then, with his long stick, he pointed to the train, which was labeled "steam engine." He said, "With this invention, we have found

a way to move heavy objects without using human or animal muscle. The steam engine helps us become more efficient. We are able to do things we have never done before."

He continued. "We are now able to go faster and farther. We can carry larger and larger loads across our great country."

He tapped on the picture of the steamboat. "Steam engines move large vessels like this steamboat." He tapped the picture of the train again and said, "Steam engines help power trains."

Then he drew a picture of the train tracks that the trains glided along on. He told of railroad stations that had been built across the country in recent years. Mr. Simpson had the younger children name the different jobs one could have working for the railroad: conductor on a train, stationmaster at the station, and engineer.

"Now it's possible to carry cattle, grain, and other cargo over land in a very short amount of time," he said. "Mark my words—one day you'll be able to travel to Florida in the course of just a week."

My little brother sat in the first row in the front of the classroom. His hand shot up. My heart quickened. What was my little brother going to say? He was seven years old and he was always asking ridiculous questions. I hated to think what might come out of his mouth this time.

"Yes, Samuel. What is it?" Mr. Simpson asked, focusing his attention on my little brother.

"Does the Underground Railroad carry cattle and grain?"

My heart felt like it might stop beating. Had Samuel heard these words in our home? Did he learn them from other children?

I wanted to shush Samuel, but I didn't dare. Someone might become suspicious about my family's involvement. Instead, I silently hoped Samuel would not say another word.

But I didn't have to worry. Mr. Simpson's face hardened. He tapped his cane on the floor.

"Has anyone else heard of this Underground Railroad?" Mr. Simpson asked sharply. A few hands in the class rose meekly.

"People may speak of a railroad that runs underground, but such a railroad is against the law."

Mr. Simpson scanned the room and added, "No one in this law-abiding Pennsylvania community or in this country should dare to break the law. Any more questions?"

Samuel looked puzzled, but he put his hand down.

The look on Mr. Simpson's face kept Samuel from continuing the discussion. Our teacher turned back to the chalkboard and wrote the word, "TRANSPORTATION." He tapped on the word with his cane and said, "We will study the lesson that is at hand. And that is transportation. Who can tell me how one can travel from New Orleans to Kansas City?"

Mr. Simpson continued lecturing about steam engines, but his words floated away from me like wisps of smoke. It would be comforting to think that everyone shared my parent's belief that slavery was wrong. The reality was that many people did not. Now I understood even more clearly why my family was in so much danger.

4

A Precious Sack
of Potatoes

We continued to keep our secret from Samuel. One night in late October, dinner began like any other meal. My mother, my father, Samuel, and I all heaped our plates full of roasted chicken, fresh baked biscuits, butter beans, and mashed potatoes. Samuel didn't notice that before we sat down to eat, my mother had prepared a separate plate, which she later took into the parlor. By then I had realized there must be a trapdoor that led down to the cellar.

Minutes later she reappeared, and we all sat down and ate. I knew that we had a dinner guest who was eating alone in the cellar.

Mother was worried about something because she ate in silence and had a concerned look on her face. Midway through dinner, my mother put down her fork and motioned for my father to follow her into the living room. I heard them talking excitedly in whispers, and I wondered what was going on. Samuel didn't notice anything unusual, and continued eating mashed potatoes as if he hadn't eaten in a week. I stopped chewing and strained to listen to their discussion. All I could hear was concern in my mother's voice and my father's reassuring tones.

Then they both returned to the dining room, sat down, and finished the meal. I looked at both my parents, but their faces no longer showed any emotion.

Later, after we finished the apple cobbler, my father spoke to Samuel. "Did you enjoy those potatoes your mother prepared tonight?"

"Yes, Papa!" he said, wiping a bit of cobbler from his face with a napkin.

"I would like you to run an errand for me," my father said.

"Oh, good!" Samuel clapped his hands. He always liked to run errands.

I looked outside at the dark skies. Samuel was too little to be out at night, so I said, "Where is Samuel going, Papa?"

"I want to send Grandpa some of our best potatoes," he told us.

"May I go, too?" I asked. I liked going to our grandparents' house and thought it would be a great adventure to walk there in the dark.

"Sorry, Amelia, but this is a job Samuel must do alone," Mother said quietly.

A short time later, my father led our old mare, Gwendolyn, to the front door. I peered out the front window and wondered why Samuel was going on the errand. I was very responsible. Samuel was only a baby. How did he earn the right to go instead of me?

Then I noticed that Gwendolyn had an oddly shaped bag draped over her back. It must be the bag of potatoes, I said to myself. I thought about our visitor in the cellar, and an idea began to take shape in my mind. Was that a bag of potatoes or a person? It looked like a bag of potatoes, but it could be something else.

Grandfather was a doctor, and his office was inside his house. He and Grandmother lived on this side of Kennett Square, only a block from the center of town. Our mare made this trek often. She would predictably walk slowly over to Grandpa's house and back, with no guidance at all from Samuel.

Papa gingerly placed Samuel behind the mare's neck and tied the reins to hang limply over her mane. The bulging bag was sagging behind him. My father slapped Gwendolyn's backside, and the old mare walked down the road with steady, slow steps. The darkness engulfed them, and they were gone.

I felt it wasn't fair that Samuel got to go, and tears began to well up in my eyes. I held them back and told myself there had to be a reason. That was when my father said, "Amelia, please come into the kitchen and sit down."

I did what he said.

"Do you know what kind of cargo Samuel is carrying?" he asked.

"Yes, Papa." My eyes were full of tears, but I had stopped myself from crying. "I know."

"Your mother and I feel that you are old enough to know what is going on and the danger we face. This afternoon we had an injured man come to us for help. He stepped into a bear trap in the woods, and his foot is badly hurt. We had to get him to Grandpa's as soon as possible. The slave master has a crew of slave catchers who are combing the countryside looking for this man. He needed immediate attention that only your grandfather could give him."

"Do the slave catchers know he's injured?"

"No, and that's to our advantage."

"A conductor brought him to our house, but it's clear he cannot go on unless your grandfather treats his injury."

"Will he stay there?"

"We hope so. Your grandfather needs to take care

of him for a few days until he can be moved again. Then we'll try to care for him as best we can."

"But why couldn't *I* have taken him to Grandpa's house? Samuel doesn't even know about the slaves coming to our house!"

My father smiled. He said quietly, "It's *because* Samuel doesn't know. He's so little that people in town will take no notice of him on our old mare. They will just think he is a small boy going to his grandpa's. If someone asks him where he's going, he will say he's taking a sack of potatoes to his grandfather's house. He won't tell the truth because he doesn't know the truth."

"I could have done it!"

"Perhaps you could have. Just the same, we thought it was best to send Samuel. No one would suspect a seven-year-old boy to be carrying a slave on the back of a horse. They might suspect a wiser eleven-year-old girl."

I knew what Papa said made sense. And yet, I longed to do more to help the slaves escape. I hoped one day I would get that chance.

5

A Family Trip

It was a glorious early winter's day. On that Saturday morning, my family and I loaded up food and blankets onto the buggy and set off for my cousins' house north of Wilmington, Pennsylvania. The day was beautiful, and I looked forward to a fun-filled afternoon playing with my cousin Maggie. Mother and Papa sat in the front of the buggy, and Samuel, Grandmother, Grandfather, and I sat in the back, singing songs. We passed by neighbors' farms and then traveled past unfamiliar fields and through thick forests.

To occupy us during the long trip, my grandfather made a scavenger list for us—a list of assorted things for us to spot alongside the road. We got points for each thing we spotted, such as: two points for a rabbit, three points for a tree hit by lightning, one point for each cow, five points for a man carrying a sack, five points for a family of four sitting on a front porch, and two points for a deer. By the time we were up to fifty points, Maggie's house was in sight.

A Family Trip

Our cousins had heard the buggy approaching, and were all waiting outside on the front porch to greet us. Paul, who was seventeen, stood waving in the doorway. Maggie's pigtails flew behind her as she ran toward the buggy. Her five-year-old brother Jessie followed her in short strides.

Not much later, we were feasting on grilled lamb chops, roasted potatoes, baked beans, mustard greens, whole-wheat biscuits, and pumpkin pie. After we finished our dinner, the boys left the dining room to play ball outside.

It had been months since Maggie and I had seen each other. We put on boots and escaped to the privacy of the familiar woods behind her house. The forest was a special place for us. As small children, we had built imaginary log cabins with logs and sticks and rocks. We imagined ourselves to be pioneer women, and set about surviving in the wilderness. We gathered berries and water and we raised a family of dolls. We helped our imaginary husbands keep the fires going, shoot game, and plant the corn. We were too old now for such childish games, but the memories of them still held a certain magic for us.

There was a well-worn path down to the stream behind the house and, beyond that, a spring that had not yet frozen solid. We carefully jumped from rock to rock, finally resting on the other side. We walked upstream, past the rock where we once saw a snapping turtle, and past the "clay pit," as we called it, where we once molded pottery into shapes we imagined the pioneers had used.

Further upstream was the spring, where we often drank its clear water. Still hanging on a branch of the oak tree beside the deep pool was a large gourd dipper. Maggie dipped the yellow gourd into the water and threw the first dipper of water in the brush behind us. Then she dipped again, this time deeper, and scooped out another dipper of water. She held the dipper to me. The water tasted as sweet as if it had honey in it. Then I dipped the gourd into the water once more and handed it to Maggie. We had done this each time we visited the spring. It had became our ritual of friendship.

Then Maggie asked, "Are your parents letting you go tonight?"

"Go where?"

She said with surprise, "You don't know why your family came to visit?"

I felt embarrassed and said, "No. Tell me."

"Our parents are going to the meetinghouse in town," she said. "Wendell Phillips from Boston is here to speak against slavery, and everyone in the county is turning out for it."

I was confused. Why hadn't my parents mentioned this to me? But I only said, "Who is Wendell Phillips?"

"Just the best speaker against slavery there has ever been and possibly ever will be. People are coming from miles around to hear him speak."

"I want to go!" I said quickly. I wondered to myself why I hadn't been told about the importance of the visit. And why did Maggie know?

"Well, we won't get to," Maggie replied. "We have to stay home with Grandmother and help her look after the boys. Paul will get to go, I imagine, but we're considered to be too young."

"We're old enough to be trusted with the safety of our brothers. Why aren't we old enough to hear a great speaker?"

"I'm not a parent," she said dryly. "I'm just reporting what I heard."

I immediately felt betrayed. My parents knew how much I believed in the work they were doing. Why wouldn't they allow me to go to the meeting?

"Let's ask them if we can go," I said, running back down the path. I didn't have to hear her reply, because as I ran quickly through the woods and brush, I heard her light footsteps right behind me. As we approached the house, I heard Jessie crying. We tiptoed inside and saw my aunt holding him in the rocking chair, softly cooing to silence his cries.

"He has an earache," she said. My uncle stood behind them, and looked at Jessie in alarm.

"He seemed fine an hour ago," I said.

"It comes on quickly like this each time," my aunt said without looking up. "He ran in crying and hasn't stopped since."

My aunt turned to my father and Uncle Horace and said, "I can't go with you tonight. I must take care of Jessie."

My mother quickly added, "I'll stay with you."

Before I could think, I blurted out, "May Maggie and I go with you, Paul, and Uncle Horace?"

My father looked troubled, and he shot a look at Uncle Horace. Then my uncle said, "We think it best that you not go."

"Oh, please!" I begged. "We will behave in the best possible manner!"

My father said, "This is a speech for adults, not children."

"Gerald," my mother said softly, so she wouldn't disturb Jessie, "I think we should let them go."

Everyone turned to stare at my mother.

"I don't know, Sarah. There might be trouble."

"They are both young ladies and very sensible," my aunt said.

My grandfather added, "This will be an event they will not likely forget. They will have a front-row seat to witness history."

I looked at Maggie, and she looked back at me. We looked at our fathers, and they nodded.

We were going!

6

A Memorable Night

We bundled up for the ride to the meetinghouse, because the night temperatures had dipped below freezing. Maggie and I huddled together under a blanket, but we were shaking from excitement rather than the cold. As we approached the hall, we saw a group of people gathered outside.

We had arrived early, so it was not too crowded inside the meetinghouse. But once people began to arrive, I realized why my father had worried about letting Maggie and me go. There were a few women, but most of the people were men. I looked for people I might recognize, and I did see a neighbor who owned a farm near our home. His name was Rawlins Mumford.

Mr. Mumford made me nervous whenever I saw him. It was hard to put my finger on why, but I knew he and my father were not good friends. They weren't enemies, but whenever I saw them together, I was aware that they were almost too nice to one another. One thing I was certain of—my father didn't trust him, and he certainly didn't like him. I knew my father's gestures well, and when I saw him hold his lips tight and fold his arms across his chest, I understood that Papa didn't like what he saw. He did this every time he saw Rawlins Mumford.

Mr. Mumford was standing near the door in the back, huddled with five other men who looked unhappy and angry. I shifted my attention to the people around me. Everyone was sitting nervously, waiting for the speaker to appear in the front of the hall. Soon the hall was so crowded with people that newcomers had to stand. The heat of all the bodies filled the building and I forgot the chill of the air outside.

Finally, the crowd was hushed and a man I didn't know introduced the speaker, Wendell Phillips. From the moment Mr. Phillips took the stage, I could not take my eyes off him. He had an intelligent but kindly face. He stood tall and erect on the stage, dressed in a long dark coat with matching trousers and glossy black boots. His shirt was starched and pressed and was a brilliant white. He wore a black bow tie and a black vest. He looked like my father did when he dressed up on Sunday morning or when he went to Philadelphia on business.

As Mr. Phillips began speaking, one of the men

standing with Rawlins Mumford interrupted him by yelling, "Question!" How could the man have a question if Mr. Phillips had not yet spoken a complete sentence? It seemed as if this man wanted to upset the speaker and pull him off course before he even began.

But the men in the front seats stood and yelled, "Let him speak! Go on, Mr. Philips!" The murmurs in the crowd lessened, then all was quiet.

Mr. Phillips' eyes moved across the crowd. He smiled and began speaking with confidence. During his one-hour speech, he never read a word from the notes in front of him. His speech seemed to have been written in his heart. He spoke with enthusiasm and intelligence. I didn't understand much of what he said, but I could not take my eyes off him, nor did my attention to his voice ever waver.

He spoke with great feeling about the American Revolution, and how the patriots long ago fought for freedom. He said that the antislavery movement was its own revolution.

Then I remember he said, "Revolutions are not made; they come. A revolution is as natural a growth as an oak. It comes out of the past. Its foundations are laid far back."

At this, there were loud mumblings, and ten men stomped out of the hall, the door slamming behind them. I noticed that Mr. Mumford was among them.

The hour passed quickly, and everyone listened breathlessly to the speaker. In closing, Mr. Phillips said that some people believed the antislavery movement would never have any effect. He argued that this was not the case. He said clearly, "No matter where you meet a dozen earnest men pledged to a new idea—

wherever you have met them, you have met the beginning of a revolution."

The crowd stood to cheer and applaud Wendell Phillips as he left the stage. I looked at Maggie's face, bright and beaming. I imagined mine looked the same. Our eyes locked, and we knew Grandfather was correct. We were witnessing an important chapter in our country's history.

7

A Warning

It was a cold January. Acres of frozen farmland stretched in front of our house, and the big oak trees seemed to be taking a long winter's sleep. It was so cold at night that our dog Gus came into the house to sleep. I shuddered to think what it might be like to sleep outside during this time of year.

Darkness came quickly, making the nights long. After school I helped my mother with chores. Then after dinner my mother and I would knit woolen sweaters, hats, and socks. I tried to imagine the person who might wear one of these garments, and I was grateful for the opportunity to help that person keep a little warmer.

Then one week, Uncle Horace came to visit and stayed a few days. My father and uncle worked hard in the downstairs bedroom sawing, hammering, and nailing. As I peered into the room, I noticed they had taken up the floorboards, exposing the earth below. The next day they carved a hole in the ground a little bigger than the size of a bed mattress. Then they lined the hole with pine planks and tent canvas to keep it dry.

My father explained to Samuel and me that this cave-like box was a secret hiding place in the case of an emergency. Samuel didn't question this explanation, but I could imagine what its use would be. About four people could lie down comfortably in the space.

When Papa and Uncle Horace finished creating the box, they replaced the floorboards. They fit so cleanly back into the space, it was difficult to see that they had ever been removed. Uncle Horace put a tiny spring underneath the boards. After the boards were securely fitted back into place, he put a thin file in a tiny hole. The board popped up. My uncle beamed. His invention worked!

I never saw any of our night visitors, but I recognized the signs that they were present. My mother prepared large amounts of food and disappeared with it before we sat down to eat. Muffled, almost unnoticeable sounds came from beneath the floorboards of our parlor. One day I investigated the parlor, looking for a trapdoor or secret panel that led downstairs, but I could see nothing.

Whenever Samuel noticed anything unusual, one of my parents would think of an excuse like, "We're making dinner for your grandparents," or "That raccoon must have gotten into the cellar again."

Months had passed since Samuel had taken the slave to my grandfather's house to recover, and although my brother often asked questions, he didn't seem to be suspicious of the answers. My parents and I were careful to speak in code to one another.

When I asked my mother what had happened to the potatoes that Samuel had taken to Grandfather's, she smiled and told me that they had arrived safely, and they had all been taken care of. I didn't know where the man had gone after his recovery, and I assumed that was for the best. If I didn't know anything more, then there was nothing I could tell anyone accidentally.

Then one day my life changed forever.

At school on Monday, we spoke of the possibility of an ice storm. A storm like that meant we would miss a few days of school. It had been raining on and off for days, and it seemed to be getting colder and colder. After I got home from school, I noticed that the slow drizzle had turned to snow.

That evening, Papa brought home emergency

supplies in case of a storm. I noticed that there was much more food and many more blankets than we would ever need for ourselves. As we climbed into bed a few hours later, I looked out the window. It was still snowing.

Excited that we might miss a school day, Samuel and I woke up the next morning before the rooster crowed. The thin morning light shone on the tiny flakes that were falling and sticking to the ground. We raced upstairs to the cupola on the top floor of our house. From the four windows, we could see all around the house. Past the road in front of the house, white fields stretched for miles. Green spruce trees that separated the fields were laced in white. The trees in the woods behind the house were also blanketed in snow.

Then we spotted them. Five riders were coming from town in a rush, their horses galloping furiously. The horses' hooves left ugly brown tracks in the snow, like mud tracked onto a clean kitchen floor.

I didn't like the angry way they were riding toward the house, so I grabbed Samuel's sleeve and ran downstairs. Papa and Mother were still sleeping, so we bounded into their room and told them we had visitors.

"Are they armed?" my father asked.

I had seen rifles strapped to their saddles. "Yes," I said breathlessly. "Something's wrong! What is it, Papa?"

My father didn't answer, but instead pushed his way to the window. He started to pull on a pair of dark pants, but Mother said, "No, Gerald, don't get dressed. We mustn't act any differently than we usually do. I think it's best to stay in your nightshirt." My father grunted and threw down his striped shirt on the bed.

"I'm not facing that crowd without my pants on, I can tell you!"

Papa instructed us to go back to bed, and hastily went downstairs. My mother looked worried, and as she got out of bed, she said, "Do as he says! Back to bed—now!" She ran down the steps and then looked back at us.

"Samuel, I need you. I want you to pretend to be sick. Can you do that?"

"Why? I'm not sick," he said.

"I know. But some men are coming to the house. I want you to play make-believe. Pretend you've got an earache."

Samuel agreed and went downstairs with Mother, and I stayed upstairs to wait. I was worried, but I hopped back into bed, pulling the covers over me.

Being warm was comforting, but not knowing what was going on was torturous. So I slipped to the front window and peeked out of the lace curtain.

A loud knock on the door shook the house. Then I heard a voice that sounded like Mr. Mumford's. He was the neighbor who had stood with the crowd of rowdy men the night that Wendell Phillips spoke.

"Open up, Turner!" Mr. Mumford shouted.

My father is not one to flinch, so he replied, "What do you want, Mumford? What do you mean coming here this time of morning?"

"You know very well what we're doing here!" Mr. Mumford said. "A family of slaves has escaped from Harold Strickland's plantation in Maryland. We hear they're headed straight this way!"

I thought hard. I hadn't remembered any noises the night before. Could there be a family below? Were we, in fact, hiding them right at this moment? Were we in danger? Was there another family in our cellar who was in danger as well?

"Who are these men?" Papa asked Mr. Mumford.

"These here are slave catchers working for Harold Strickland. There's a bounty for those slaves, and they've tracked them up this way. Slick crowd, they are, but we're getting them this time for sure!"

"I still don't see how this concerns me."

"Turner, I saw you at the Wendell Phillips lecture. We know where your loyalties lie."

My father said calmly, "Yes, I do believe that all men are created equal, as our constitution states. Slavery goes against the constitution. It's not right for us to keep any man or woman in slavery. And I believe that it's not right to sell any goods that are made from slave labor."

Papa had always told us to keep our opinions to ourselves. I was surprised that he expressed himself so boldly to these men. I wondered how far he would go.

"Then you admit you are hiding Harold Strickland's property?" Mr. Mumford asked.

"I admit nothing of the sort!"

Mr. Mumford ignored Papa's denial. "Now, Turner, let's be civil. I'm here with these gentlemen because we're neighbors. I told them I knew you and could persuade you to give us the straight story. You aren't going to make a liar of me, now are you?"

"I haven't seen any slave family," my father said.

"Gerald," I heard my mother call from the parlor, "could you get the fire going?"

"If you will excuse me," I heard my father say, "my wife needs help."

A dark, tall man with the eyes of a hawk addressed my father. "Mr. Turner."

Papa turned back and stared at the stranger.

The man said, "If you know something, you better tell us now. It will be easier on you if you just tell us what you know. If you don't, you'll regret it. You *and* your family."

"I'll not have you threatening me or my family! I have done nothing wrong, and I have to ask you to leave us be!"

"That so?" he asked menacingly. "Then you wouldn't mind if we came in and took a look around your house?"

My father hesitated a minute and then said, "No, I don't mind. I have nothing to hide. You can come in and look all you want. Just don't disturb my children."

I peeked over the stairway railing and I saw the men shuffle inside with my father. First they went into the living room. Then I heard them walk into the parlor, where my mother was in the rocking chair with Samuel on her lap.

"Good morning, Mrs. Turner," Mr. Mumford said, tipping his hat.

"Morning, Mr. Mumford," she said back. She kept rocking. Then she said to Mr. Mumford, "The boy needs some heat if he's going to get well."

"Yes, ma'am, we'll be finished soon," he said. And then I heard my father tossing firewood in the fireplace. Soon the smell of burning wood wafted upstairs.

Footsteps echoed through each room, and occasionally the slave hunters tapped on a wall or floorboard. Then I heard one of them come toward the stairs, and I hopped quickly in bed and closed my eyes as if I were asleep.

The men didn't linger long upstairs. They peeked into each room, and thundered back downstairs.

"How do we get into the cellar?" the tall man asked.

"This way," my father said, and he led them to the cellar door at the side of the house. After he unlocked the padlock, they climbed down inside the cellar. Seeing nothing but a stone wall, old tools, and canned goods, they climbed right back out.

Then they all walked to the front porch. After ten or fifteen minutes, they huddled together and spoke softly. I strained to hear what they said to my father, and I think I heard, "Sorry to have bothered you."

"Not at all," my father said. He had a wonderful ability to be pleasant, even when he was very angry.

Lack of evidence and his tone must have satisfied the men, because then they left.

8

Getting Ready

It snowed lightly all that January day, but the clouds above became dark and threatening. There was enough snow to keep us home from school, but not quite enough to have fun playing outside. Because of the storm, many people were expected to load up with supplies at the general store, so Papa opened up before seven o'clock. Sweet smells from the kitchen told me that Mother was baking muffins.

I asked Mother if I could help my father at the store.

"No, Amelia," she said. "Not today. I need your help." I looked at the kitchen table and saw that my mother had stacked up a pile of sweet squash, a bag of flour, milk, and dried beans. A large uncut ham was also on the table. We might be preparing for company that night.

I eagerly sat down to peel and cut away the hard shell of the squash, thinking about the sweet orange treat that was to follow. Then I put the squash in a large pot to boil. Later I would mash it with nutmeg and butter. After that, Mother let me make biscuits as she set the lima beans to boil, which she seasoned with big chunks of ham. On the stove, a corn chowder was stewing. We worked quietly and purposefully.

A few hours later we heard Gwendolyn snorting, alerting us that Papa had arrived home in the buggy. He had filled it with more supplies, and we both ran out to help him unload.

My father looked more concerned than I had ever seen him. He turned to my mother and said sharply, "Be sure the lantern is lit in the front window."

"It always is," my mother answered.

It was then that I was certain we were expecting more visitors that night.

"Why do the slave catchers go after the runaways?" I asked my father.

"It's a way to make money, Amelia," he replied. "Slave catchers can make a lot of money when they catch and return a slave."

"How much money?" I asked.

"Sometimes one hundred dollars. Sometimes two hundred. I've heard of one slave catcher who earns six hundred dollars a year just catching slaves and returning them to their masters."

Six hundred dollars a year! I was amazed. That was a lot of money.

"And what happens to the slave when he goes back to the master?" I asked.

My father didn't answer, so my mother said, "Go ahead, Gerald. Tell her."

"A slave might be sold," he said quietly. "Or beaten. Or both."

"And how much does a slave cost?"

"I'm not sure, Amelia. Maybe twelve hundred dollars. It depends on how healthy the person is and what kind of work the slave can do."

It was difficult to understand. How could people place a value on a human life? It was then that I began to truly realize that sometimes laws and customs weren't fair. It was up to people like us to change them.

9

Houseguests

There were many signs that we were to have night visitors. It might be a flash in my father's eyes as he spoke to my mother. It might be the early arrival of my father at the end of the day. Or it could be the anxious watching at the window and the extra cooking. This time, Mr. Mumford and the slave catchers alerted me that a runaway family might appear at our door.

Before we went to bed that night, the storm that had been predicted was beginning to rage. Winds howled, and the snow began falling fast and furious. I wondered what was happening to that family during such a storm, and if they would ever reach our house.

By the time we went to bed, there were already six or so inches of snow on the ground. I lay in bed, trying to sleep, but also wondering how much snow we would find the next morning.

I listened carefully and lay awake for a long time, but heard no familiar "Who's there?" at the doorway.

Finally, I was so tired from the day's work that I fell into a deep sleep.

The next morning, snow was still falling when I awoke. I ran past my parent's bedroom, but I noticed their room was empty. Sounds drifted up from the kitchen, and I wondered what time it was. I climbed the ladder up to the cupola and looked at the ground below.

I had never seen so much white powder in my life. The dirt lane that led past our house had disappeared, and I noticed that snow had drifted onto the front porch and covered it. Trees were drowned in it, with only the tip-tops of the smaller ones peaking through. In some places, I could see drifts of twelve feet or more.

I climbed back down into the hallway and peeked into Samuel's room. He was snoring lightly, and when I peered closer, I saw that his cheeks were flushed. He must have sensed I was there, because he opened his eyes and smiled. "It's cold," he said sleepily.

"Go back to sleep, then," I said, and I pulled the quilt above his shoulders. "I'll call you for breakfast."

Mother and Papa were fully dressed, and I joined them in the kitchen. Mother was making biscuits and Papa was making a pot of coffee. Bacon was frying in the pan, and a stew of potatoes and onions was simmering.

Mother said, "I worry about their being cold. And it's always damp. Not a place for two children. Not to speak of being very crowded down there."

My father didn't look at me as he spoke back. "I think it's safe to let them come up and eat properly."

"The night visitors?" I asked quickly.

"Yes," my father said seriously.

"How long do you reckon we'll be snowed in?" my mother asked.

"It could be a few days or even weeks," my father answered. "There's no telling. Depends on the weather. If it stays cold, who can say? If it warms up, there's still no way to predict. One thing is sure—no one will be moving around very much in this snow."

"Perhaps we should just move the family upstairs with us," my mother suggested.

"I think it'll be all right to do that," Papa agreed.

"So you mean we'll all be together?" I asked in excitement. Then I remembered my brother. "Samuel, too?"

"Yes," my mother said. "Samuel will have to learn to keep our secret. We'll just have to trust him."

"Samuel can do it," I said in support of my brother. I wasn't completely sure he could be trusted, but there was no way we could have the family inside our living areas without letting Samuel in on the family secret.

"I agree," my father said. "I'll go get them now. Would you like to come with me, Amelia?"

My heart raced as I followed my father into the parlor. He quietly lifted up the rocking chair that stood beside the fireplace and put it to the side. Then he pulled back the rug. Underneath it all was a trapdoor, just as I had suspected. Once the door was pulled up, Papa got a ladder to climb down into the cellar, the same place the slave catchers had once searched.

My father climbed down, and I followed. A faint light from a lantern lit the space, and I saw a man and a woman speaking quietly to each other. On a mattress beside them lay two small figures. They stirred when my father spoke.

"We think it best that you come upstairs," my father told them.

The father of the children stood and spoke, his rich, deep voice filled with concern. "It is safe to do this?"

"Yes. The snow is at least four feet deep outside. No one can move. Not you, nor the men after you. You are quite safe, and we wish that you would come upstairs where you will be more comfortable," Papa replied.

He added, "We just need to rearrange the cellar so that if it is ever searched again, it doesn't look like a hiding place." Then he tossed the mattress on its side, placing old lanterns and tools in front of it. Before long, it looked just like an odd combination of junk.

Then I tugged on my father's coat. He remembered me and said, "This is my daughter, Amelia. Amelia, this is Mr. Jeremiah and Miss Mary. The children are Obie and Rebecca."

"Hello," I said shyly. "I'm pleased to meet you."

"Hello," the two adults said back.

"What's your last name, Mr. Jeremiah?" I asked.

Mr. Jeremiah shot a glance at his wife, and she said, "We haven't chosen one yet."

He paused and Miss Mary asked me quietly, "What is your family's last name?"

"Turner," I said.

"Then we will choose Turner to be our name. What do you think, Jeremiah?" Mary said in an accent that was new to me.

"Turner is a fine name," he replied. Then he spoke to me. "But you can call us Mr. Jeremiah and Miss Mary."

I blushed and thanked him.

Mr. Jeremiah turned and spoke softly to the boy and girl. They rose slowly from the cold floor. When they stood up, I was almost too startled to speak. The boy was Samuel's age, and the girl appeared to be a little younger than me. The boy was dressed in baggy trousers, at least two sizes too big. The girl wore a dress of dark, heavy cotton and woolen tights underneath. They were both skinny as sticks, and they both wore coats that loosely hung over their clothes.

The boy rubbed his face, and the girl's alert eyes looked sharply at me and then away.

I spoke again. "My name is Amelia. We want you to come upstairs and have breakfast. My mother is cooking biscuits, bacon, and potatoes. I imagine she has eggs, too!"

The girl and boy looked at their mother, and she said, "Get along, now!" With their heavy clothes still on, they followed me up the ladder and into the parlor. As they stood in the kitchen waiting for their parents, they turned slowly around in circles, staring at the room. They said nothing.

Samuel chose that moment to come bounding down the stairs, and he stopped short when he saw the two children.

"Who are you?" he asked brightly.

"Obie and Rebecca," I said. They still stood together and didn't make a sound.

10

Teacher and Student

I don't think I've ever seen a hungrier pair of children than Obie and Rebecca. They ate their breakfast slowly and carefully, savoring each morsel. When my mother piled on more potatoes and biscuits, they kept eating. They were both so small. I wondered how they could eat so much. Finally Miss Mary said, "Stop, children. You'll get mighty sick if you eat too much."

After breakfast, my father and Mr. Jeremiah decided it was safe enough to shovel a clear path to the woodpile, the well, and the barn. Mother asked Rebecca and me to feed the chickens and gather the eggs. Mother hadn't milked the cow yet, so Rebecca said, shyly, "Do you want me to do that? I used to do it every day."

Mother looked surprised and handed her the pail. "If you like," she replied.

There was a lull in the storm, and Rebecca stopped outside the back door and put her hand on the snow.

She picked some up, and then she giggled and looked at me sideways.

"You've never seen snow before?" I asked.

She shook her head as she patted some snow into a ball.

"Do you like it?"

She nodded. I scooped up a handful of the cold, fresh snow. I said, "After you milk the cow, we can use some of the creamy milk and snow to make ice cream!" She nodded in agreement, but I realized that she had probably never had ice cream, so she didn't know what I meant.

As if to speed us along, the storm picked that moment to rage once more. The wind whipped against our faces as we worked our way along the shoveled path to the barn. We went slowly, protecting ourselves from the storm by closing the barn door. Without hesitating, Rebecca sat down on the stool next to the cow.

She said in a slow but sweet southern drawl, "I like doing this. It keeps my hands warm."

I watched her expert hands milk the cow. The warm milk quickly filled the metal pail. Steam rose from the frothy milk and Rebecca's breath froze in the air. She leaned her head gently against the cow's side, just as I had seen my mother do countless times. Her strong, skinny arms moved skillfully and efficiently. Suddenly, I felt like a child. I knew very little about life and hard work. She seemed to know a world I had never experienced.

"How did you learn to do that?" I asked. I had tried to do it before, but the cow had stomped and complained. My mother had laughed, and said it was faster if she took over. I hadn't tried again.

"It gets easy after a while."

"I don't know," I said doubtfully.

"If you do this every morning, you learn pretty quick. And if you don't get milk, you get into a heap of trouble!"

She looked up at me and added, "I can show you how to do it."

"Mother tried. I was no good at it."

"You can try again some time. I'm a good teacher. I teach Obie how to do things all the time."

After she finished, the cow shifted and snorted gently. Rebecca picked up the full pail of milk and set it aside. Then together we gathered a basketful of fresh eggs. One hen was not happy about being disturbed, and my face was too close for her comfort. The hen reared her head back and rudely pecked me on the nose. I jumped back and cried out in surprise. Rebecca giggled, then covered her mouth. I rubbed my nose and giggled with her. I should have known better than to crowd the hen.

As we were leaving the barn, Rebecca pointed to two small, old pairs of snowshoes hanging on the wall. "What are those?" she asked.

I got an idea. I pulled down the two child-size pairs of shoes, the ones Samuel and I used to walk in the snow. "Watch me," I told her.

I strapped one pair of snowshoes to her shoes, and then said, "You can walk in the snow in these."

She waddled around on the straw and giggled, "Not very well!"

I put on the second pair and said, "It's easier in the snow. Come on, I want to show you my favorite place."

Then we walked out into the snow and climbed up on the small bank. I walked ahead, slowly making my way. I looked back and saw Rebecca standing there. "Well, come on!" I said.

She climbed up on the bank, and slowly walked into the soft snow as if she expected to sink any moment.

"The shoes spread out your weight," I explained. Then we walked to the back of the barn and into the forest, and I noticed that her legs had finally gotten the hang of it. The wind had slowed down, and we walked quietly into the still woods. Snow hung heavily over the evergreens, and occasionally the wind would blow a drift in front of us. No animals were about— no doubt they were keeping warm somewhere, and were staying away from humans. We walked for about a quarter mile to a large outcrop of rock, a place where Maggie and I had often played last summer. The snow sloped down toward an opening, and I leaned onto the rock and unstrapped my snowshoes. I stood in the opening and gestured for Rebecca to follow me. Inside I showed her my secret cave, a crude but cozy place that only Maggie and I knew about. Inside was just as I had left it. There were wooden logs for seats and a doll's china teaset. A small table with a tablecloth was in the middle of the room, and a vase filled with dried daisies still sat on top.

"It's nice," Rebecca said.

"We had better get back," I said. "Mother will wonder what happened to us, and besides, we have the eggs and milk to take inside." So we put our snowshoes back on and I added, "We can come back and fix it up tomorrow, if you want to."

"Yes, let's come back. We can fix it up really nice."

So we walked back to the barn, gathered the milk and eggs, and scooped up a large bowl filled with snow. Back in the kitchen I showed her how to make ice cream by adding vanilla, cream, and sugar to the fresh white snow. Obie and Samuel were playing jacks in the parlor, and we called them into the kitchen for the treat.

By this time, Rebecca was used to the snow, and she silently ate the creamy treat. Obie, however, didn't know what to make of the cold ice cream. He put his finger in it and drew it back. When he saw Samuel eating it, he picked up his spoon and ate hungrily. Pretty soon, we had finished the whole batch, and Mother promised to make more after dinner.

Papa and Mr. Jeremiah were out shoveling and tending to the animals, and our mothers were busy tidying the house and preparing the bedrooms for sleep that night. Mother and Miss Mary were working together to make up the bed in the downstairs guest bedroom. Obie and Samuel were playing a wild game of tag with our dog Gus and were running from room to room. They were having a grand old time.

On days when school was closed because of bad weather, my parents always made me do schoolwork. Because we had visitors, I thought today might be different. I stepped into the bedroom and asked my mother about our schoolwork. "Our chores are done. Should Samuel and I do our lessons now?"

My mother looked at me and said, "Enjoy yourselves. Go play in the parlor with Rebecca."

I thought about Obie and Samuel, now playing a game of hide-and-seek. It would be more fun to play upstairs, away from the noisy boys. "May we play in my bedroom?"

"It's too cold in there," my mother said. All our bedrooms had fireplaces, but we rarely used them, except in the most severe conditions. "I'll have to make a fire first," she added.

"I can make a fire," Miss Mary said.

"We'll take up the wood!" I said.

"All right, then, but don't leave wood chips on the stairs going up," Mother warned.

A half hour later, the fire was roaring, and Rebecca and I sat in front of it as we waited for the heat to fill the chilled room. Outside, the storm was still blowing and gave no sign of stopping. We sat on the floor, hugging our knees. Gus snuggled in between us, and finally flopped on the floor and went to sleep.

Then Rebecca said quietly, "This is the first time I've felt safe in a long time. Everything is so nice here."

I was surprised. Why would she say something like that?

Then she added, *"Yawa."*

"What did you say?" I asked.

"*Yawa,*" she repeated. "It means having everything you need. It's what you have here."

"I've never heard that word before."

"It's a word used by the Hausa people, my mother's ancestors."

"Do the Hausa people live in Africa?" I asked.

"Yes," she replied, and then was silent.

The fire crackled and we sat for a moment. Then I asked, "How did you get here last night?"

"We walked from the last safe house. We had expected to be here two nights ago, but we knew the slave catchers were right behind us. So we went back to the safe house. We hid there for a day, then came here. We were told it'd be safe because the slave catchers had already been here." Then she said, "They'll be back, you know."

"If they do, you'll either be hidden or long gone." Then I quickly added, "I'm glad you're here now."

"Why?" she asked.

"I'm happy to have someone to play with. I usually have to play alone—unless Maggie is here. She's my cousin. She knows about the cave, too. You would like Maggie. She would like you a lot, too."

"How do you know?"

"I like you, so Maggie would like you."

The room was warm now, so we got up and began to play. First we dressed up in fancy clothes and hats—clothes my mother had passed down to me to play with. Then we chose dolls to care for and dress. Then I suggested we play "school."

"How do you play school?" she asked.

"One of us can be the teacher, and one of us can be the student," I said. "We can take turns teaching each other. I'll be the teacher first."

I gathered up my schoolbooks, paper, and a chalkboard. I wrote the letter "A" on the board. "What is this letter?" I asked.

Rebecca looked at the letter. She said, "I don't know."

I was surprised. Was she pretending, or didn't she know the alphabet? *"A!"* I said. I wrote *Rebecca.*

"Do you know what this word is?"

She again said, "I don't know."

I studied her face and then realized she didn't know her letters or how to read! I said, "This is your name. *Rebecca.* It begins with *R.*"

She put her finger under her name and said softly, "Rebecca."

"Why can't you read?" I asked. I knew she was smart. It didn't make sense.

"I never learned," she said simply. "They wouldn't let me go to school. My daddy says it's against the law for slaves to read."

I was amazed at that fact, so I asked, "Do you want to learn?"

"Will you teach me?" she asked.

"Of course I will!" I cried. What fun that would be, teaching someone else to read!

"Are you sure it's all right?" she asked uncertainly.

"You'll be free soon. You'll need to learn how to read. Why not start now?"

So we sat down by the fire and I began to write the letters of the alphabet. I taught her each one, and gave her a picture underneath each one to help her remember. *Apple* for *a, ball* for *b,* and *cat* for *c.* She was a quick learner, and spent the better part of the afternoon learning the sounds and letters of the alphabet. Then I read her one of my favorite fairy tales, "Jack and the Beanstalk." She listened to each and every word, and after I finished, she took the book and stared at it. I guessed she had never held a book before.

"Did this really happen a long time ago?" she asked.

"Oh no! I don't think so."

"Why do you like this story?"

I thought for a minute. "I don't know. Maybe it's because Jack is just a small boy who outsmarts a terrible giant. I like the idea that no matter how small you are, you can overcome something that's big and evil."

"I like this story, too," Rebecca said. She seemed deep in thought, and she suddenly added, *"Dakasuwa."*

"Is that another Hausa word?" I asked.

"Yes. It has different meanings. It can mean 'to teach one another.'" She sat there looking at the fire and added, "I can teach you something."

"You're going to teach me how to milk the cow," I reminded her.

"Oh, anyone can do that," she said. "I'll teach you a song that I learned from my mother."

Then she began to sing:

Follow the drinking gourd,
Follow the drinking gourd;
For the old man says,
"Follow the drinking gourd."

When the sun comes back,
When the first quail calls,
Then the time is come.
Follow the drinking gourd.

The river bank is a very good road,
The dead trees show the way.
Left foot, peg foot going on,
Follow the drinking gourd.

The river ends between two hills,
Follow the drinking gourd;

Another river on the other side
Follows the drinking gourd.

Where the little river
Meets the great big one,
the old man waits—
Follow the drinking gourd.

She stopped singing and said, "That is a song of freedom. And it's a song of secrets."

"Secrets?" I asked.

"Yes," she said. "The words have special meanings. 'When the sun comes back' and 'when the quail calls' tell you when to leave the plantation and go to freedom."

"A quail calls you?"

"Yes, but it's not a real quail. It's someone making the sound of a quail."

She was silent for a moment. Then I asked, "What does 'the drinking gourd' mean in the song? I know that a drinking gourd is a cup made from a gourd. You cut out the round part of the gourd and use the long neck of the gourd as a handle."

"Think of places where you can see a drinking gourd," Rebecca responded.

I thought. I had seen drinking gourds hung up on

branches next to springs where drinking water was pure and sweet. I searched my brain for other places a drinking gourd might be seen. Then I remembered that "dipper" is another word for "drinking gourd" and that there is a dipper formed from stars in the sky.

I said excitedly, "In the sky! The drinking gourd is the Big Dipper!"

Rebecca nodded and said, "The Big Dipper points north to the North Star. It points the way to Canada."

I asked, "What about the 'peg foot'? And what does that have to do with keeping secrets?"

In quiet tones, as if someone were listening, she said, "There is a peg-legged sailor named Peg Leg Joe. Peg Leg Joe is a free man, and he travels all around the South. Sometimes he stops and does odd jobs on the plantations. He blends right in with everybody else, so the slave masters never notice him. He talks to the slaves and teaches them how to escape. And the song tells what Peg Leg Joe teaches."

"And the slave masters can't figure out what the song means?"

"I guess not," Rebecca responded.

"That's incredible!"

"After Peg Leg Joe leaves a plantation, some slaves disappear and never return. I guess the directions are good enough, because I've never heard of any being caught."

"Have you ever seen Peg Leg Joe?"

"No, I've just heard about him."

"Where did Peg Leg Joe go to help the slaves?"

"I'm not sure. Some people think it might be Alabama," Rebecca replied.

"Have you ever been to Alabama?" I asked.

"Is Alabama between Maryland and here?"

"Not exactly," I said, and I took out a map. I showed her the state of Pennsylvania. I put my finger where we live. Then I showed her Reading, Chester, Lancaster, and Philadelphia. I outlined the state of Maryland and asked her where she lived.

"I'm not sure," she said. So we traced from my house back to the Maryland border. I showed her the Susquehanna River and asked her if she remembered crossing it.

"Oh yes! We rode a ferry across. We traveled with a family who pretended we were their slaves."

We studied the map. No matter where she had come from in Maryland, the amount of miles was amazing. I looked at her in admiration. Imagine traveling that far on foot!

"Where do you usually stay?" I asked.

"Sometimes in people's barns or in their cellars. But most of the time, we sleep outside in the woods."

"At night?"

"No! We travel at night. We usually sleep during the daytime. Except last night. We got in early and slept in your cellar."

"How do you keep from being discovered?"

"Someone always keeps watch."

My thoughts went back to Rebecca's song. "What about the dead trees in the song? What does 'the dead trees show the way' mean?"

"Think about what you find on dead trees."

"Bark," I thought. Then I said, "And moss."

"That's right, moss. The north side of the tree doesn't get sun, so the moss grows there. So if it's a cloudy night, and you can't see the Big Dipper, what could you use as a guide to go north?"

"A dead tree that has moss on its bark!"

"That's right. The moss tells you which way is north."

"But what about the little river and the big river?" I asked, my heart racing in excitement.

"I guess they would be between Alabama and Canada," she said.

We looked at the map. I pointed, "Okay. Peg Leg Joe would start in Alabama. Then go up." I studied the map. "It could be the Ohio River. Perhaps the little river is the Tennessee."

She ran her finger along the two rivers. "It doesn't look so far on a map does it?"

I smiled. "No." I showed her the key. "Each inch stands for fifty miles." She just stared at the map, as if to try to understand it all.

I wanted to know more about Rebecca's journey, so I asked, "Who helps you as you go along? Does your father lead the way?"

She explained that their conductors changed as they moved from place to place. The conductor they had now was a free man who lived not far from here. Now he was at home with his family, taking care of them during the storm. Since he was a former slave, others watched his every move, and he felt it wasn't safe for Rebecca's family to stay at his house. Rebecca didn't tell me the conductor's name, and I didn't ask.

"How did you find your first conductor?" I asked.

"We started without one."

"Tell me about how you started out!"

"We had a map. It wasn't a map like this one, it was a special map. You see, only a few of the slaves ever get to go into town or leave the plantation. So it's hard to know what the land is like outside the farm. But my father is a blacksmith, and sometimes he was sent to another plantation to work. Our master hired him out, just like he hired out my mother and me."

"What did you and your mother do?"

"We kept house. We did the wash and cleaned the house. I ironed. We brought water in. We made sure the floors were always shiny. My mother cooked."

"Was it hard?"

She replied, "I guess so."

"What about Mr. Strickland? Was he a bad man?" I asked breathlessly. I was almost afraid to ask about him. I had heard so many horror stories about the terrible things slaves had to endure.

"He was all right, as masters go, I suppose. We got enough to eat, and we always had warm clothing. But times were getting bad. He was losing money and was selling off slaves right and left. That's why we left. We knew he was going to split our family up, sure as anything. Mamma and Daddy wouldn't stand for that, so we decided we had to make a move."

"Just like that?"

"Oh no. Mamma and Daddy had been thinking about it for a long time. Mr. Strickland's crops were getting worse and worse, and each year he'd sell off a slave or two to make up for his losses. Then he started gambling. He was in debt to so many people, we knew our time together was not going to last."

"Tell me about your map," I asked.

"Years ago, my mamma started making a quilt. It

was white and quilted with red, green, yellow, and blue threads. After Daddy would go somewhere off the plantation, he'd come back and draw her a map of where he went. Then she quilted that part of the map on the top of the quilt with colored threads. By the time she finished it, we had a map of the whole county. We knew where all the hills were, where the water and rivers were, and where all the farmhouses were. Mamma and Daddy knew the marks on the quilt by heart, and that's how we were able to escape."

"Where is the map now?"

"At the plantation, for others to follow."

"Where did you go first?"

"Mamma and I met this friendly white woman on a road into town one day. Out of the clear blue, she pulled us over and said to us, 'If you ever need help, you can come to me.'"

"So when we left the plantation, we walked straight to her house. Then she told us where the next safe house could be found. We walked five miles the first night. That's how we got on the Underground Railroad."

"Was it scary leaving?" I asked.

"Yes. We left on a Saturday night, because we wouldn't be missed until Monday morning. That gave us two nights to travel before anyone followed us."

"You only traveled at night?"

"Mostly." Then Rebecca reconsidered. "No. One time we were out in the light. That day we carried farm tools as if we were on our way to work. But my father thought two children together with them might make people suspicious. After that, we stayed hidden during the day."

I thought about all she had told me. Now the song would make sense. "Would you sing the song again for me, now that I know what it means?" I asked. Rebecca sang quietly. As she sang the last line, her mother appeared at the door.

"Rebecca!" Miss Mary said sternly. "You know you mustn't sing that song here!"

"But, Mamma," she protested, "Amelia is my friend. She is teaching me, and I wanted to teach her."

Miss Mary's face softened. Then she said quietly, "I understand. But secrecy is our best friend. This is a song that we must keep to ourselves. Not only to protect us, but the ones that come after us."

"I'm sorry, Mamma," she said.

After Rebecca's mother left the room, I said, "I know your mamma is right. You should keep that song to yourself. As for me, I've already forgotten it."

11

Snowbound

The next day the sky and snow created a canvas of white and blue. The snow was so bright we had to shade our eyes as we walked to the barn to milk the cow and gather eggs.

By now the path to the barn looked like an open tunnel with walls that were almost as tall as Rebecca. I stood in the tunnel and found that I was only two inches taller than the banked snow. I knew that we were snowbound, and no amount of shoveling would change that. Rebecca and her family would be with us for another week, at least.

My father said that the snow had to melt enough to walk comfortably in before the Turners could be followed. Even then, we would have to cover their tracks with those of the horses. Carrying the family in the wagon was a better idea, but the wagon couldn't move until the snow melted. Then there was the problem of mud and ice. But I tried not to worry about their leaving. All I wanted right now was to enjoy the snow, the sunshine, and their company.

Papa and Mr. Jeremiah dug out the paths to the barn and well once more. Obie and Sam played chase with the dog. Then they began digging paths of their own. Obie said he wanted to make a snow puzzle, so he and Samuel dug twisting paths in the snow.

Before we gathered the eggs, Rebecca showed me how to milk the cow. I struggled at first, and the cow stomped and grunted. I looked up at Rebecca in frustration.

Rebecca said, "Don't think too much about what you're doing. You're doing the cow a favor by taking the milk, so just do it."

I closed my eyes like I had seen Rebecca do. Then I pulled, and milk began flowing, in small squirts at first, then bigger and bigger. The cow relaxed, and so did I. I opened my eyes and looked up at Rebecca in surprise.

She said, "Don't look at me! Keep going!"

Soon my hands felt sore and tired, but I didn't dare stop. Now that I had learned how, I was determined to keep going until the cow had given all the milk she could give. Finally, Rebecca said, "You're done." I sighed in relief. I couldn't have lasted another second.

On the way back to the house, I got an idea. I suggested that we gather the boys and make a snowman.

"What's a snowman?" Rebecca asked.

"A man made out of snow," I laughed.

Moments later, the four of us were rolling big balls of snow. Rebecca and I rolled the large ball for the bottom of the snowman. We pushed the large ball until we could not push it any further, and there it sat on the ground. Samuel and Obie made a smaller ball for the upper body. Then we helped pick up the smaller ball and lifted it on top of the bigger ball and patted them together.

I told the boys to make a smaller ball for the head, and Rebecca and I went inside to gather materials for the clothes and face.

"What if we make a snow woman instead?" she asked.

I thought about it. "A fine idea!" I said.

We went inside and gathered our materials, asking my mother for some of the more unusual items. Then we went back outside. Samuel and Obie were placing the head on top of the second ball.

Then Rebecca took over. Before long, we stood back and took stock of our creation. There she stood proudly, our snow woman. She had two twigs for arms, a carrot nose, charcoal eyes, and eyebrows made of raisins. But what made her special were her red lips made of cranberries and hair made of orange yarn, which we had covered with a bright blue hat. She wore Mother's old yellow apron and a purple scarf around her neck. She looked warm as toast!

I looked back at the window and saw our mothers. They were standing at the kitchen window and sipping hot drinks. They were chatting and smiling, and I liked to think they were sharing in our pleasure of a job well done. Rebecca looked up at the window in fright, her muscles tense. I asked her what was wrong.

She relaxed and said, "Oh, nothing. Mr. Strickland didn't like me to play. If I was caught playing, I got punished. For a minute, I was scared when I saw the grown-ups watching me."

I didn't have much time to think about what she said, because at that moment Samuel began throwing snowballs at us. Then Obie joined in, and soon all four of us were pitching snowballs back and forth. Rebecca and I moved to one side of the yard and began building a snow fort. Obie and Samuel began building one of their own. We played for another hour, and the time passed quickly until Mother called to us to come in for stew.

I carried a bowl of beef stew up to Mr. Jeremiah, who was in the cupola, keeping watch. My father and he took turns doing chores and keeping watch. We had to be careful, in case the slave catchers tried to travel through the snow.

After lunch we all sat together at the kitchen table. Mother said that since school was temporarily canceled, we would attend school at home each afternoon. Thus we began a day of study. Mother asked me to write an essay on "Friendship," which I gladly did, since I had a new friend to write about.

Mother put Samuel to work on addition problems on the abacus. Obie looked on, and Samuel helped him count the colored beads. Then Samuel showed Obie and Rebecca how to write numbers. After I finished writing my essay, I read it aloud to everyone. Rebecca smiled. I think she was pleased.

Then she said, "I want to read."

"But you have to know your letters first!" I said quickly.

"I know them," Rebecca said. Then she recited the ABC's from beginning to end.

"I just taught them to you yesterday!" I said in amazement.

"I only have a few days to learn. I've *got* to be fast!" she responded.

Mother and I made cards for her. We printed a word on a card, and if it could be pictured, we drew a picture on the back. We printed the words *like, the, an, cat, dog, horse, was, were, ran, Rebecca, Amelia, jumps,* and *hides.* Then we asked her what words she wanted to learn. She said she wanted to learn *freedom, North Star,* and the names of her family members. I held up the cards and Rebecca said the words after me. Then we mixed up the cards and put them in an order that made a sentence. Rebecca was so excited. After an hour, she could actually read a sentence! I have never seen anyone so happy to read a few words.

Then I remembered. I did know someone who was that happy to read. That person was me. I had felt exactly the same way when I had read my first sentence.

12

Icy Weather

The week passed quickly. It stayed cold for a few days as everyone dug out of the snowy white mess. Then midweek, the temperatures soared and we even played outside without our coats and hats. On Friday, a northern wind blasted down upon us. The snow wasn't as deep, but it had turned into hardened blocks of ice. The fields around our house looked as though they had been covered with a thick white layer of frosting.

The snow had stranded Rebecca's family for days. Travel was still impossible with the dangerous ice on the roads, in the fields, and even outside our kitchen door.

Papa and Mr. Jeremiah continued their watch and kept up the outside chores. Mr. Jeremiah fixed the hinges on an old door for us, and both men kept a steady load of firewood coming inside.

As for us children, we continued to study. Now that I knew Rebecca wanted to learn so much, we spent the morning on schoolwork. Obie had learned some of his letters, and he had even learned how to add a few numbers.

Rebecca amazed me. She had an excellent memory and a talent for reading. She was reading as well as I did in my first year of school! She was also beginning to write. At first her handwriting was clumsy and messy, but her writing improved every day. I enjoyed helping her.

In the afternoons, we walked out to the cave using our snowshoes, and began cleaning it up and adding homey touches. We took old blankets and wrapped our dolls in them to keep them warm. After an hour of playing, we snuggled under the blankets ourselves until we got warm once again. One day we replaced the dried flowers with holly and fresh cedar, draped cedar boughs over the entrance, and put a fresh tablecloth on the table.

By nightfall, we were tired after all the play and chores. Hungry as wolves, we gulped down our dinner. After we washed and put away the dishes, we listened to Papa read fairy tales like "Beauty and the Beast" or "Cinderella" in front of the fire.

Then, ten days after the Turners had arrived, the weather turned warm again. Icicles were melting and water was dripping off the roof in little streams. Everywhere I walked, I could hear water flowing underneath the ice and snow. That day Papa got up early in the morning and said he would check on my grandparents to see how they were getting along. They were both in good health, but still my father worried. Then Father said he wanted to check on the store. He didn't expect anything to be out of order, but I think he just missed going to the store every day.

The ice was still too dangerous for our mare, Gwendolyn, to make the trip, so Father walked the two miles to the store. I watched him take a step on the ice, and then another step. The ice broke, and he sank into the snow. He would go another two or three steps on top of the ice, and then sink down. He plowed through the ice-encrusted snow, and I could almost feel the sweat beading down his back as he struggled along.

I returned to the kitchen and settled down to my lessons along with Rebecca, Samuel, and Obie. While my mother taught us, Rebecca's mother prepared a beef and barley soup. From time to time, she would look over and listen to the lessons. I wondered if she, too, wished she could learn with us.

Then we heard the sounds of heavy boots clomping down the stairs. It must be Mr. Jeremiah coming from the cupola.

"Miz Turner!" he yelled. "A man is coming!"

My mother did not hesitate. "Don't panic," she instructed us. In seconds, she took charge and told us what to do. It was a good thing, too. A man was looking closely at the icy tracks in the snow and mud in our backyard. Gus was barking furiously at the man circling the house. For the man who approached the house on foot was none other than Rawlins Mumford.

13

The Secret Box

Mother led Obie, Rebecca, Mr. Jeremiah, and Miss Mary into the downstairs bedroom. She lifted the rug to show the wood flooring. She knelt down with a thin file and slid it into a small hole. A board lifted up slightly, and she pulled it easily from the floor. Then she removed four other boards to reveal the secret box, just large enough for four people.

"Here!" she said nervously. "Quickly!"

The family climbed carefully inside the box and Mother covered them quickly with the boards and the rug. Then she waved Samuel and me into the kitchen. Mr. Mumford was banging on the door, and Mother walked slowly to the door and opened it.

"How are you, ma'am?" I heard Mr. Mumford say to my mother.

"As well as expected, I suppose," Mother replied.

Samuel and I were sitting at the kitchen table as if we were doing lessons. I was reading the story "Tom Thumb," looking for spelling words. Mother was giving me a spelling test today and I was trying to make a list of words she might choose to test me on. Samuel was drawing a picture of our house with a pencil. A pot of cider and cinnamon sticks brewed on the stove.

"May I come in for a moment, Mrs. Turner?" I heard Mr. Mumford say.

"Yes, of course!" she said in a friendly way. "Come in and have a cup of hot cider. But I'm sorry to say that Gerald is not here right now."

"Over at the store, is he?"

"Yes, I'm afraid so."

"Well then, I will take a cup of that cider and then be on my way." He sat down on a kitchen chair near our table. We nodded to him, and I pretended to continue my lesson.

Mr. Mumford's eyes quickly scanned the kitchen. Then he craned his neck to look into the parlor and stared at Mother's rocking chair. Quickly, he turned his head back into the room and caught me watching him. I looked down, and he looked out the window. Then I looked at Samuel. He was staring at Mr. Mumford. I wanted to warn Samuel not to speak, but I didn't dare say anything. I silently wished: Please, Samuel, don't give us away!

My mother handed Mr. Mumford a cup of

steaming liquid. He said, "Never did catch that family of slaves."

"Is that so?" my mother replied, as if she were not interested.

"Can't figure out what happened to them. It's like they just disappeared into thin air. Like that snow outside. Soon it'll be melted enough so we can start tracking again."

"Why are you helping the slave catchers, Mr. Mumford? Don't you have more important things to do?" Mother asked.

He scowled at my mother and answered, "I'm just upholding the law, that's all. Trying to get a man back what is rightfully his."

He sipped the cider. "I bet you know just how safe those slaves are, don't you?"

My mother gripped the chair. "I don't know what you mean."

"Well," he said, "those tracks out there. I see two sets of men's boots. Not just the one set that Gerald's boots would make. And there sure are a lot of children's footsteps. Looks like a heap of people been moving about in that backyard."

"You have a big imagination, Mr. Mumford. My husband has more than one pair of shoes, you know."

"Two different sizes?"

My mother didn't respond. She said, "If you suspect something, you can look around all you want. We have nothing to hide."

"You wouldn't mind if I looked in your bedrooms and cellar?"

"Of course not! You'll see how ridiculous your claims truly are."

Mr. Mumford turned to Samuel and said, "What about you? Hiding any people around here?"

I froze and looked at Samuel. Would he give away the secret?

My fear turned to shock when I heard him reply, "If we were, we surely wouldn't tell you, now would we?"

My face gave nothing away, but I smiled inside. Samuel had just talked back to an adult, and the secret was still safe!

Mr. Mumford replied, "No, I don't suppose you would."

He took his hat and put it on his head. He said, "I'll bid you good-bye."

My mother stopped him and said, "No, I would like for you to search the house before you leave. I would like you to leave my home fully satisfied."

Mr. Mumford pulled off his hat. "Very well," he

said. And then he looked in each and every room, checking under beds and even peering at the ceiling. Then he walked to the kitchen door.

Mr. Mumford shut the door behind him and walked to the back of the house. He brushed off the snow and chipped off the ice from the cellar entrance. Then he pulled up the cover to the cellar door. He stepped down into the darkened basement. He climbed back up and looked back into the sunshine. He made his way to the barn, and after disappearing inside for fifteen minutes, he came outside and left. He stared at the house and studied the tracks frozen on the path. My mother opened the door and said, "Good day, Mr. Mumford."

"Good day, Mrs. Turner." He added, "I guess I was mistaken. Please accept my apologies." Then he walked back toward his farm.

As soon as Mr. Mumford was out of sight of the house, Mother rushed to the bedroom. Samuel and I followed and helped her throw back the rug and remove the boards. One by one, Rebecca's family climbed out of the box. My heart was beating fast, but I didn't need to worry. They appeared fine, and we had all narrowly escaped detection. All was well, for the moment.

14

A Plan

Later that afternoon, the weather seemed to be getting warmer, but heavy clouds covered the sky. Rebecca and I stopped our lessons and peered out from the cupola where Rebecca's father was keeping watch. We were both glad to see my father coming toward us, struggling through the ice. He was carrying a large, odd-shaped bundle in his hands, and I wondered what it could be.

I ran outside to help him carry the package, and I found that it was very light.

"What's inside this, Papa?" I asked.

He grinned at me. "It's a plan of escape for our friends." He looked up at the dark clouds overhead. "Now all we need is a little snow to make it work."

On the short way back to the house, it began to snow. Papa seemed almost cheerful, especially considering what had happened that day. I told him about Mr. Mumford's visit, but he wasn't as bothered by it as I would have expected. He just seemed determined to get back to the house.

Once inside, he gathered everyone together and announced that Rebecca's family was leaving that night.

"Why so soon?" my mother asked.

My father pointed to the snow outside. "This is the most unpredictable weather I have ever seen. Even the old timers have never seen anything like it. But I think that the weather is acting as our friend."

He set the bundle on the table and said, "For ten days we have been blessed with Mr. Jeremiah and his family." Tears began to gather in my eyes as I listened to him.

"We have worked together. We have played together. We have shared many meals, and we have become true friends. But now it's time for us to part."

"But how, Gerald?" my mother asked anxiously.

My father didn't answer, but instead unwrapped the light but awkward package. As he pulled away the strings and brown paper, I held my breath. What could be inside?

Papa held up four pairs of snowshoes. The large flat shoes were made of wood and string and had leather straps that held a boot on top. Papa explained that the snowshoes would help the Turners to escape over thick snow. There were two large pairs for Mr. Jeremiah and Miss Mary and two smaller pairs for

Obie and Rebecca.

"Do you think Obie is able to wear snowshoes?" my mother asked.

"I can do it if Rebecca can!" Obie said firmly. Everyone laughed, and no one doubted his word.

"But the snow is covered with a sheet of ice!" Mother interrupted.

Papa smiled. "Not for long. From the look of those clouds, there will be plenty of snow for good snowshoeing."

Mr. Jeremiah held out his hand to my father. "How can I show you my thanks?"

"You already have," my father replied, grabbing Mr. Jeremiah's hand.

It was at that moment that we heard a knock at the door. Our faces froze, and the image of one man on the other side occurred to each of us: Rawlins Mumford. No one moved, and the knock came again—this time more timidly.

My father went to the door. "Who's there?" he asked.

Then we heard the familiar reply, "A friend."

My father opened the door, and there stood a stocky man who seemed to be much older than my father. His arms were strong and muscular, and there was a look of determination in his broad face. His skin was much darker than Mr. Jeremiah's, and there was a little graying in his neatly trimmed beard.

"Thomas Stephens!" my mother said in relief. "How did you ever make it all the way here?"

"I started out after breakfast," he said. "There is no

time to lose. We must be moving on, because they are closing in on you. The slave hunters could be back this evening."

"They've already come once," my mother said.

"They won't give up until they find the family. They'll be back," cautioned Mr. Stephens.

"It's a good thing you came to the store today and we hatched this plan," my father said.

Mr. Stephens nodded. "Tonight then?" He looked at Mr. Jeremiah and Miss Mary. They nodded in agreement. "Tonight," they said together.

15

A Sad Farewell

There was not much preparation to be done for the departure. Rebecca's family could not carry bags of clothing or bundles of food because such provisions would mark them as runaways. Packing too much would also slow them down on their journey to freedom. So they set off with only the clothes on their backs and some ham and biscuits.

Once they left us, they might walk or they might be carried in a wagon. They might hop on a train and travel as passengers. They might ferry across a river or lake. Whatever route they took, it would be a long journey to Canada. They would have to travel north through Pennsylvania, across New York, and most likely pass by Niagara Falls before they crossed the border into Canada.

As I thought about her trip, I became excited for Rebecca. She was about to have a new life in a new country. I hoped for her safe passage to Canada, but I was sorry to lose a friend. Would I ever see her again?

I led her up to my room, and we sat on the bed. I

wanted to give her a gift, but I was uncertain as to what she might be able to carry. I said, "I want you to take something that will remind you of me." Then I looked at my book of fairy tales, the book we had spent many hours reading.

I handed it to her. "Is it too much for you to carry?"

She smiled. "If it weighed a hundred pounds, I would carry it with me."

I wrapped it in a brown cloth and tied it with a blue ribbon. I handed it to her. "Don't forget me."

She took the bundle and asked, "How could I?" Then she put the book in a large pocket in the lining of her coat.

We didn't have a chance to say anything else, as Mr. Jeremiah called for us to come downstairs. We both clunked down the steps and saw everyone standing at the door. My father was handing out rubber coats to keep the rain and snow off their wool clothing. Then we walked outside and stood in the blustery weather. At least a foot of snow had already fallen, and more was coming. There was plenty of snow for snowshoeing—almost too much.

I helped Rebecca strap on her snowshoes. Papa and Samuel helped Obie. With each passing moment, the storm got worse. The wind picked up and bits of sleet flew sideways, cutting my cheeks like knives. Obie struggled in the shoes, and I knew the conditions were too rough for them to get very far.

My father said to Mr. Stephens, "It's too stormy to leave. Come back inside!"

"No!" Mr. Stephens yelled over the wind. "We'll be discovered! They'll be coming tonight! Unless you can hide five of us, we must go."

We all knew that the space in the bedroom would only hide four people, so the Turner family had to go north. Suddenly an idea hit me, and I called out to Papa, "They can make it to the cave!"

"What cave?" my mother asked.

Rebecca and I looked at one another. "There's a small cave about a quarter of a mile into the woods."

"I think I know the one you mean," my father said.

"It's between the stream and the large piling of rocks. Maggie and I found it. Rebecca and I have been playing house there," I said. "It's plenty big enough for the Turners and Mr. Stephens."

"Can you get there by yourself in a storm?" Papa asked.

"Gerald!" my mother scolded. "Not in this storm!"

"There are only two small pairs of snowshoes in the barn," my father said. "It'll have to be Amelia.

Only she knows exactly where the cave is."

I tried to convince my mother. "I can do it, Mother! I've been walking in the snow for days. I'm really strong. Besides, I know the shortest, fastest way to get to the cave. I could get there blindfolded."

My mother put her hands on my shoulders. "All right," she said. "Please be careful."

"Take Gus with you," Papa suggested. "He knows the way back home, no matter where you go."

I could tell by the look on my mother's face that she didn't want me to go, but she said nothing. I gave her a hug. "Don't worry, Mother."

She hugged me and said, "I will worry. But you go on. And get back as fast as you can!"

Before she could change her mind, I strapped on my snowshoes, and we walked toward the forest in single file. Obie followed me, and Rebecca walked behind him. Rebecca's mother followed her, and Mr. Jeremiah and Mr. Stephens kept up the rear. The only one of our group that had no trouble making it through the snow seemed to be Gus. His long legs hopped in and out of the snow, the ice below it supporting his slight body. His breath was heavy, but he seemed to be smiling. Just looking at him gave me confidence.

A Sad Farewell

I took short steps so Obie could easily step into my tracks. He walked behind me like a little soldier. The wind wormed its way into my thick coat, so I pulled my wool scarf tighter around my neck. I looked back and saw Rebecca behind Obie. Soon I forgot the cold, concentrating instead on how well my snowshoes worked. There was a thin layer of ice below the snow, and it was frozen solid. My weight was equally carried on the strings and frames of the snowshoes. Each foot fell down an inch or two in the deep snow, then stopped. Still, it was hard work, and my face was soon red with the hard work of walking.

Finally, the large collection of rocks was straight ahead, framed by the leafless trees around them. A lone cedar tree stood at the entrance of the cave. I walked steadily and slowly toward it. The snow died down until it disappeared altogether inside the opening. As the others caught up to me, I unstrapped my snowshoes. The next thing I had to do was to make sure some animal hadn't beaten us to the cave. Gus put my fears to rest as he slid inside, stood straight up, and wagged his tail. If there had been an animal inside, he would have known.

I stooped down and stuck my head inside. My eyes adjusted to the lack of light, and I stared at the home

Rebecca and I had made days before. The tablecloth and the flower vase were still there as we had left them. It wasn't warm, but it would do.

Moments later, Mr. Jeremiah, Miss Mary, and Mr. Stephens came inside. Miss Mary said simply, "We have stayed in much worse."

Mr. Stephens looked at me sharply and said, "You best get back now."

I paused, and Mr. Jeremiah said, "You're in enough danger as it is. Take your dog and go back home!"

"Won't you be cold tonight?"

Miss Mary said kindly, "We've slept out during much colder nights than this."

Rebecca said, "Besides, we have blankets!"

"But . . ." I said, reluctant to leave them.

Then Rebecca hugged me and said, "We'll see each other again. I promise."

I looked at her and smiled. Then I hugged them all. I strapped on my snowshoes and climbed up the slope outside the cave. I dared not look back, for fear that I wouldn't have the heart to return home. What would happen to them next?

As I walked back toward the house, I realized that there were no snowshoe tracks to give away the escape. I stopped and watched the tracks I had just made. Within a minute, they were covered with a light dusting of snow. In five minutes, no one would know I had been there. The Turner family would be safe. I began walking faster and faster toward home. I was ten feet away from the back door when I saw a group of men standing inside the front doorway. Before they saw me, I took off my snowshoes and hid them behind the well. I walked toward the house, and recognized Rawlins Mumford and the four slave catchers.

I hopped up the front steps onto the porch and waited for the men to let me pass. Gus rushed past me and ran inside the house. I looked Mr. Mumford straight in the eye, and he said, "Where have you been?"

"Getting the dog inside. It's too cold for Gus to stay in the snow."

Without giving me another thought, the men walked out the door. Their search for the family of four escaped slaves would continue. My heart swelled with pride that I had just helped them escape. Once the men were gone, my father closed the front door, and we all breathed sighs of relief.

The Turner family was out of our hands now—they were once again passengers moving on the Underground Railroad.

Epilogue

I would like to think that once you make a friend, that friend is yours to have always. I believe that time and distance shouldn't destroy or weaken a friendship. But in some ways, the ten days I spent with Rebecca and Obie and their family became somewhat of a dream. I couldn't tell anyone—not even my cousin Maggie. In the following years, Samuel and I were discouraged from speaking of them. Papa said that one day we might forget and say something that might give us away.

And so we acted as though we had never seen or heard of the family that had taken our name. I longed to write Rebecca a letter once she made it to Canada, if she ever did. But how were we to know if they ever made it? Even the conductor, Thomas Stephens, would not know of their fate. He only led them to the next safe house, wherever that might have been.

In the next few years, we continued to help escaped slaves as they passed our way. Some of them I met, and some of them stayed so briefly that I never even saw them. After they left our home, we never knew what happened to them.

We did hear some stories of slaves who had escaped to safety. We heard of the amazing Harriet Tubman, a conductor on the Underground Railroad. She was a slave who lived in Maryland. Her master hired her out to a woman who was cruel to her, so Harriet decided to escape to freedom. Her two brothers agreed to go with her, but they soon turned back in fear. She continued on and found passage on the Underground Railroad. Once she escaped to freedom, she did not rest. She returned again and again, and we heard stories that she led almost 300 slaves to freedom. Because she was a well-known conductor, there was a $40,000 reward for her capture, dead or alive.

We heard no stories about the Turner family. They were just a few of the thousands of people who bravely tried to escape the bonds of slavery. Unfortunately, there was no way to know what had happened to them. They might have made it, and they might not have.

In 1859, I began to teach children to read at the school in Kennett Square. Ever since I had taught Rebecca the basics of reading and writing, I knew it was what I wanted to do.

In November of 1860, President Lincoln was elected president of the United States. In December,

South Carolina decided it no longer wanted to be part of the United States. Not much later, six other states decided the same thing. Together they formed a separate nation called the Confederate States of America.

Then we had two countries instead of one and everything changed. On April 14, 1861, the Civil War began. The northern states were fighting the southern states. The war lasted almost four years. Finally, on April 9, 1865, it ended. All of the states were united once again in a single nation. That same year, slavery was outlawed forever.

A year after the Civil War ended, I met a handsome young man. Two years later we married, and I got a teaching job in Philadelphia that I kept for the next twenty-five years.

When I was twenty-eight, I had my first child, Jennifer. A year later, my son Nicholas was born. Randolph came next, followed by baby Patricia. In the meantime, my brother Samuel had married and gone into the lumber business and worked with my father and mother to expand our family store.

My children grew up, and I became a grandmother. I had not forgotten Rebecca, but with the passing of time, I thought about her less often.

On one warm, humid summer's day, I took my

youngest grandchild on the front porch. She had just fallen asleep, and I sat down to enjoy a glass of lemonade. The baby slept peacefully in the cradle beside me as I rocked her gently with my foot.

Then I saw a tall woman and a well-dressed man walking toward me. She was about my age. She wore a fashionable dress of expensive blue cotton and a matching felt hat with a smart feather. Her walk suddenly slowed, and she began studying the house numbers. She stopped in front of my house.

"I'm looking for a woman named Amelia Turner," she said.

"I was once Amelia Turner," I said. "Now my name is Amelia Turner Graham."

We both stared at one another. Something in her face and voice reminded me of the past.

"Rebecca?" I asked in disbelief.

She nodded and a broad smile filled her face. This woman resembled Rebecca, but gone was the shyness. Before me stood a confident and attractive woman. Forty years disappeared, and we rushed into each other's arms.

"Is it possible?" I exclaimed in between hugs.

"Did you ever doubt that we would see each other again?" she asked in surprise.

"At times, I'm afraid so," I admitted. "I've

wondered for so many years what might have happened to you."

I looked at the handsome man standing at Rebecca's side. He didn't look familiar, but a person could change a lot in forty years. "Is this Obie?" I asked.

Rebecca looked at the man and laughed. "Heavens, no! Obediah is a cherry farmer in

Michigan. This is my husband, Andrew Taylor."

"You're married?" I asked. But of course, she would have married. I felt foolish, but she just laughed. "Did you think I was going to stay a small girl forever? I have three children who now live in Boston. One is a teacher."

Rebecca's husband interrupted. "Rebecca became a teacher herself."

I was so pleased, but speechless in my delight and shock at seeing my old friend.

"You know, I have you to thank for starting me on the path to learning," Rebecca said.

"I only taught you a few words," I protested.

"They were important words," Rebecca countered.

"For the past ten years, Rebecca has wanted to find you," Rebecca's husband said.

"Did you go back to Kennett Square?" I asked.

"Yes," she said, "I saw your mother and your father. I saw Samuel and his family, too. They told me you were in Philadelphia."

Then she reached into a bag she carried and pulled out a small book I instantly recognized. "Remember this book?" she asked.

I took the book and flipped through the pages, looking at the familiar illustrations. There was Jack and the beanstalk and Beauty and her beast.

I said, "How could I forget this?"

"Remember the day you first read this book to me? You taught me a lot about new beginnings."

"And you taught me that I had something to share. I became a teacher because of you. But I have always felt that I learned the most important lesson from you. You and your family taught me the meaning of courage," I told Rebecca.

"My parents were the brave ones. I just did what my parents told me to do."

"But," I said, "you never seemed to be frightened of what you had to do."

"You had courage, too. Have you forgotten the day you took us to the cave?" she insisted.

"No, of course not," I said. "I'll never forget anything about those days."

I looked at her, standing so proudly with her husband. Rebecca was right. As children we had learned important lessons from one another. I looked down at my beautiful grandchild sleeping next to me. I tried to imagine the lessons that she had yet to learn and to teach.